The Crooked Tree

A story for kids who are going through tough times

Copyright © 2018 Emma Forsythe
All rights reserved
First Edition

Fulton Books, Inc.
Meadville, PA

Published by Fulton Books 2018

ISBN 978-1-63338-417-0 (Paperback)
ISBN 978-1-63338-418-7 (Digital)

Printed in the United States of America

The Crooked Tree

Emma Forsythe

Once upon a time, there was a hillside in the country where tall, strong trees and pretty flowers grew.

The tall trees were planted on the top of the hill and were very beautiful. They were straight and very sturdy. In the spring, the large trees enjoyed the gentle rains, and in the summer, the trees soaked up the warmth of the sun. When autumn came and the days became shorter, the leaves of the trees turned golden. People noticed them when they came to the village.

But there was another tree nearby who was not like the tall strong trees. This little tree was named Miranda. She lived on the lower part of the hill where it was dark and cool. The big trees on the top of the hill took all the sun and the rain, so Miranda did not receive as much. She did not grow as strong and as tall as the others did. Instead, she was small and crooked.

Most people didn't notice Miranda. She used to look up at the trees on the hilltop and think, "I wish that I was up there with the others. Maybe I would grow as strong and tall as they did and maybe I would be as beautiful too."

Then she would look at her small trunk and feel that she was not very pretty. She could never be like they were.

Sometimes, on quiet afternoons, the big trees would talk among themselves. The large tree on the end would look at each of the other trees to see how tall they were.

"I am the biggest tree on the hill," he would boast. "The biggest and the strongest." He was very proud of this.

"Well, I have more leaves than you do," said another tree who had many branches, each with many leaves. She was very beautiful.

"And I am the most graceful," interrupted a third tree. "I bend in the wind, and I dance in the storms."

Miranda would watch and would sometimes try to talk with the other trees, but she did not interest them. They would continue to talk among themselves and would ignore the little tree from the bottom of the hillside. "After all, she's not like us," they said.

This made Miranda feel very lonely.

Since the trees were not friendly, Miranda decided to look for other friends. At first, she thought she had found some when she saw people from the village coming toward her. "This one is too small," said the man. "We can't have a picnic under this tree."

"We have to go to the top of the hill," said his wife. With this, they left and climbed to the top of the hill to have a picnic in the soft, cool grass under the tall trees. There would be no picnics under Miranda.

But while Miranda was too small for adults to sit under, she was perfect for the children of the village. One day, a group of them were playing when they noticed the little tree. They liked her because she was small, and so were they. They would sit beneath her branches and talk or play games.

This made Miranda happy. She liked her new friends. Sometimes, the children would climb in her branches. This tickled Miranda, and she would laugh until her leaves would shake.

She began to learn the names of the children. There was Kevin who ran fast and Sarah who was very smart. Tommy was the story teller, and Emily liked to sing. Marcus would swing from Miranda's branches, and April liked to make the others laugh.

Miranda's favorite child, however, was Rachael. When Rachael would come to play, she often threw her arms around the tree. "I can reach all around this tree, so this is my favorite," Rachael would tell the others. When she said this, Miranda was very proud indeed.

Miranda also found more friends among the birds of the air who would sit in her branches. There were robins and wrens, cardinals and blue birds. She liked their chirping and singing in the early morning. In the evening, Miranda enjoyed the cooing song of the dove. It was soft and gentle, and it seemed to say, "Day is done. Time to rest. Sleep well." Miranda felt this song was best way to end the day. She would fold her branches closer to her and go to sleep.

Miranda loved the children and the birds. Without them, she would have been very lonely, but having friends made her feel good.

One day, the children did not come out because of the weather. The summer sun had been very hot, and it was uncomfortable to be outside. The children played inside, and the birds were quiet.

Miranda even found herself getting drowsy, though it was afternoon and not a time for sleep. She was starting to nap when she suddenly awoke. There was a change in the air. A storm was coming, but this was not like other summer storms. This would be a storm like no other.

Miranda tucked her branches closer to her and prepared for the storm to hit. The winds began to howl, and the sky grew dark and scary.

Soon the rain began to fall. It fell so fast that it was difficult to see anything. Hailstones began to fall from the sky. These were hard, and they flattened many of the pretty flowers on the hillside.

Bam! The first lightning bolt hit. "That sounds awfully close," thought Miranda. A loud rumble of thunder followed the lightning, and the ground shook. The wind was blowing hard.

Boom! Another strike of lightning hit and made a sizzling sound. This was followed by another roll of thunder and more lightning. Each clap was louder and fiercer than the one before.

Bang! Still another bolt of lightning hit very close by. More thunder came with it.

"I can do this," said Miranda. "I won't let myself be afraid of this storm." With this, Miranda bent into the wind so that it could not hurt her or break her branches. She dug her roots into the ground against the storm and waited for it to end.

It was Miranda's time to be brave and strong. She would not let the storm frighten her.

After a while, the storm began to move away from the village. It was finally over. The air felt cool and clean. Miranda looked to the hilltop and was surprised at what she saw there. The tall line of beautiful strong trees was gone, destroyed by lightning and wind. All that remained of the tall trees was a tangle of branches, leaves, and broken pieces of wood.

"Our tree is fine," she heard a girl shout in the distance. Could it possibly be Rachael, wondered Miranda. She turned and saw Kevin, Sarah, and Rachael running toward her.

"I'm so happy that you are all right," said Rachael as she threw her arms around Miranda's small trunk. Miranda was very happy again.

Soon the sun began to shine. A rainbow appeared in the sky. Miranda felt the sunshine on her leaves now that the bigger trees were no longer blocking it. She began to relax and enjoy its warmth. The angry storm was over, and unlike the others, Miranda had lasted.

About the Author

Emma Forsythe has published various articles in both the health care field as well as in the general interest realm. She has more than twenty years' experience as a mental health therapist, working as a mobile therapist with children and their families. She has also been active as a foster parent for Children's Services and enjoys spending time with both kids and adolescents. She lives in the Pittsburgh area.

CPSIA information can be obtained
at www.ICGtesting.com
Printed in the USA
BVHW020138161118
532961BV00017BA/636/P